Pecos Bill

The Kipling Press Library of American Folktales

Pecos Bill

★

RETOLD BY PATRICK MCGRATH

ILLUSTRATED BY T. LEWIS

The Kipling Press ★ New York

Published by The Kipling Press, Inc.
155 Sixth Avenue, New York, New York 10013
Copyright © 1988 by The Kipling Press
Text Copyright © 1988 by Patrick McGrath
Illustrations Copyright © 1988 by T. Lewis
Book Design by Michael Hortens
All Rights Reserved.

International Standard Book Number: 0-9437-1815-5
Manufactured and Printed in the United States of America

Foreword

People who tell stories about Pecos Bill don't really believe that those stories are true. They know they are telling tall tales, or "windies," about a fictional character.

People all over the world tell tall tales – or lies – often in storytelling contests, in which each person tries to tell the biggest and the best lie. But tall tales about strong outdoorsmen such as Pecos Bill are particularly popular in America. In the beginning, the stories were told aloud by one person to another. Soon people began describing a situation using Pecos Bill. For example, they might say a place was "as messy as if Pecos Bill rode a cyclone through here."

Later on, some of the stories were written down and published. They became very popular through magazines. In October 1923, *Century* magazine printed several stories about Bill in an article titled "The Saga of Pecos Bill." These stories were written by Edward O'Reilly. Twelve years later, O'Reilly wrote four more stories about Pecos Bill, with new adventures in each one. And, in the meantime, several other authors had also written stories about Pecos Bill.

The Pecos Bill stories did not come from cowboys, as many people think. Many of the incidents written by American writers are similar to other traditional folk stories from other countries and other times. For example, Pecos Bill is found and reared by coyotes, like the twin brothers Romulus and Remus in Greek mythology.

Some people wonder if Edward O'Reilly and other writers created folklike stories of Pecos Bill and then let the public think they were real cowboys tales. The writers may have thought people would like the stories more if they thought they were getting real folktales.

Heroes such as Pecos Bill were very important to such a young country as the United States. Americans had an inferiority complex because the U.S. didn't have much history yet, or many stories about their country. They needed to create some "ready-made" folktales to give the nation an identity.

So what does Pecos Bill tell us about America? He tells us that we are a nation of fearless and resourceful people who are always ready to tame the wilderness. We are like Pecos Bill because we think big and we never give up. Pecos Bill's tall tales show us we like to laugh. And they also let us laugh at ourselves whenever we laugh at him!

Sandra Dolby Stahl
Associate Professor of Folklore and American
Studies at Indiana University

Howdy, stranger! Pete's the name—

Pete the coyote. Not quite sure what a coyote is? Well, I'll tell you. We're a small cousin to the wolf, with a thick, furry coat and a beautiful, bushy tail. The prairies are our home, and prairie dogs are our favorite vittles. At night we head for the hills to howl at the moon. Have you ever heard us howling away on a moonlit night? That's our own brand of singing.

I'm here to tell you the tale of Pecos Bill, and it begins with a passel of coyotes. I should know, because those coyotes happened to be relatives of mine—my Uncle Joe's family, in fact. Uncle Joe knows

a lot of stories about Pecos Bill, and there aren't none
of 'em that aren't as true as I'm sittin' here. Uncle Joe
used to tell us about when Pecos Bill was just a runt,
no bigger than a cub, and his kinfolk moved west in a
wagon pulled by four big, strong horses. Now, Uncle
Joe told me that while Bill's kin were crossing the
Pecos River in Texas, little Bill fell plum out of that
wagon. Well, with sixteen brothers and sisters, he
warn't missed for three or four weeks, and by then he'd
moved right in with my Uncle Joe. So that's how he
grew up—with a whole pack of coyotes, by the banks
of the Pecos River.

Even as a little fellow, Bill was considerable strong,
for he took after his mama, who'd once kilt forty-five
buffalo, usin' just a broom handle. Uncle Joe told us

that when Bill was just ten years old, he got into a
fight with two mean-tempered grizzly bears. Uncle
Joe allowed as how he was worried: maybe Bill could
handle *one* mean grizzly—but *two?* Don't you know,
Bill just put his arms around those two grizzly bears
and he *hugged* them to death, and that was the end
of that.

Well, Bill was just settin' down to have a bite of
grizzly bear for breakfast, when a cowboy came ridin'
up and wanted to know why he was down on all
fours, carrying on just like a coyote.

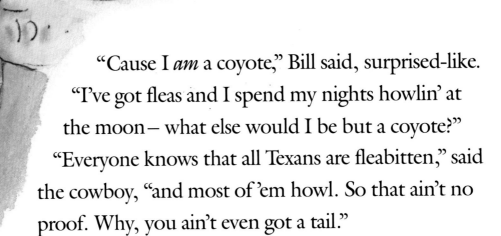

"Cause I *am* a coyote," Bill said, surprised-like. "I've got fleas and I spend my nights howlin' at the moon—what else would I be but a coyote?"

"Everyone knows that all Texans are fleabitten," said the cowboy, "and most of 'em howl. So that ain't no proof. Why, you ain't even got a tail."

"Darned if that ain't true," said Bill, after he'd looked over his shoulder. "I don't have a tail." And that's how Bill figured out he was a boy, when all those years he'd thought sure he was a coyote!

Well, soon after that, Bill left my Uncle Joe's family and went off with that cowboy, and that made all the coyotes very sad. But Bill had decided he wanted to be a cowboy, too, and it didn't take longer than the flick of a snake's eye for him to do it. Pecos Bill was the best darn cowboy in Texas. He invented the six-shooter and the bucking bronco, the branding iron and the lasso. And in his spare time, he rounded up cattle, chased train robbers, and killed so many bad men that no one could keep track of 'em. Pretty soon there warn't a whole lot left for Bill to do in Texas, so he figured he'd head further west. Uncle Joe admitted he got a little teary the day Bill came to say goodbye.

Now by this time, Bill had become a man—and what a man! He stood over eight feet tall, and his shoulders were broad as a wagon. His eyes glowed dark red, and his teeth were all whittled down to points. Nine guns and seven bowie knives hung from his belt, and when he laughed long and loud—which was often—the cattle stampeded and old ladies dropped down dead from shock. And now, Bill was headed west.

Bill didn't have an easy time of it on the journey. First off, his horse broke a leg and Bill had to travel on foot, with his saddle slung up on his shoulder. One day when he was tramping down the side of a mountain, a big old rattlesnake, ten feet long, reared up in his path and commenced to shakin' its rattle and spittin' its poison. Well, Bill put down his saddle and he grabbed that riled-up rattler and gave it three hard chomps with his pointed teeth. Right then, that poor snake had had enough and it began beggin' Bill for mercy. So Bill coiled the snake around his arm just like a rope and went on his way.

Not long after, Bill was makin' his way through a lonely canyon, when suddenly the biggest mountain lion in America—the size of four bulls, at least—sprang out at him. Do you think Pecos Bill was scared? No more'n if he had just met a pussy cat. Bill loved a good fight with a mountain lion—the bigger, the better!

So pretty soon the pair of them were goin' at it, and
the fur was flying. The sky was so full of fur, you
couldn't even see the sun. After about three minutes,
that mountain lion gave up and begged for mercy. "Stop,
Bill," pleaded the lion. "I was just funnin'. Honest!"

Bill decided he'd keep the mountain lion and use it for a horse. He saddled it up, and they galloped off down the mountain in a cloud of dust.

That night, far off in the darkness, Bill saw the light of a campfire burning. He rode up to find a gang of cowboys, gulpin' down beans and coffee. Bill helped himself to a few platefuls of beans and washed 'em down with a gallon of boiling coffee. Then he asked who the boss of the cowboys was. Right behind him, a deep, loud, nasty growl said, "I am. Who wants to know?"

Bill turned to face a huge, dusty cowboy, strong as two oxes and mad as three angry rhinos. He was a very, very bad cowboy, indeed! But after taking a long, hard gander at Pecos Bill, this cowboy suddenly changed his tune about being the cowboy boss. Maybe you can guess who took over as new boss!

So now Bill had a gang, and right away he got himself a ranch with cattle. And now, don't you think he might have settled on down to the life of a respectable cowboy? No sirree! Not Pecos Bill. Why, he had himself more adventures than ever, not leastwise finding himself a horse to replace his mountain lion. You see, that lion—the one the size of four bulls—had lit off back for the mountains, and Bill was left with nothing to ride.

Bill was hoping to find a colt, a young horse he could train. And he knew that the wildest, fastest, proudest colt in all the West was a pure white mustang that all the cowboys had been trying to capture for months. Not one of 'em had been able to lay even a finger on it.

But Bill was the craftiest cowboy of them all. He knew a water hole where that mustang went to drink, and he lay on the ground beside that hole for a solid week, so's he could lasso the colt when it showed up. When he finally roped it and jumped on its back, he rode it clear across the prairies and up and down the canyons for *another* whole week, while that colt bucked like the dickens trying to throw him off. Finally it had to admit it was bested, and then Bill talked gently to it in horse language, which he spoke as fluently as he spoke coyote.

He brought his new horse home to the ranch,
where the cowboys took one look at it and gave it the
name Widow-Maker. Bill raised Widow-Maker on raw
dynamite and nitroglycerin, and he was the only man
in America who could ride it.

Uncle Joe always said Pecos Bill could ride *anything*. Only one time Bill ever fell off—and that was the time he rode a cyclone.

Now, you know a cyclone is a windstorm that twists round and round, and snatches up anything that gets in its way, whether those things be horses, people, houses, or trees. Bill had bet good money with some of his cowboy friends that he could ride a cyclone without even using a saddle. He didn't aim to ride just any cyclone, either. He set out to find the worst twister that had ever been known, and somewhere around Kansas, he found it, lassoed it, and climbed on its back.

Off the cyclone went, clear across Texas, whirling and spinning like a top.

★ *Pecos Bill* ★ 23

Well, Bill just sat up there, slapping the cyclone's side with his hat. With his free hand, he was rolling cigarettes and lighting them up with bolts of lightning. The cyclone tipped over several mountains and quite a few forests, and tied four rivers in knots. But no matter how wild it bucked, it couldn't throw Bill off its back.

But then the cyclone got another idea. Cyclones are made of clouds, my Uncle Joe explained to me, and so they can turn into rain mighty easy. So that twister decided to rain Bill right down over California. When he landed, Bill made a great hole in the ground, more than a hundred feet deep. Today they call that big hole Death Valley.

After that, hard times lay ahead for Pecos Bill. It all came about when he decided to marry. One day Bill was skinning a few buffalo down by the Rio Grande when he looked up and saw a woman ridin' down the current on the back of a catfish. Uncle Joe reminded me that Texas catfish are bigger than whales, which meant this cowgirl was one fine rider. Slue-Foot Sue she was called, and Bill fell in love with her right there and then. And he married her just as soon as she'd have him.

But Bill and Sue didn't live happily ever after. On her very own weddin' day, Slue-Foot Sue asked Bill if he'd let her take a little ride on Widow-Maker, just for fun. What a mistake! Widow-Maker tossed Sue right off, and Sue flew so high in the sky that she had to duck her head for fear of bumpin' it on the moon. To worsen matters, Sue was all gussied up in her wedding finery—a wedding gown with a steel-spring bustle in it—and when she dropped back down to earth, she bounced right back up again, into the sky.

Up and down, up and down she went, recalled my Uncle Joe, for *three days!* Poor Slue-Foot Sue! Poor Pecos Bill! With tears in his eyes, Bill finally had to shoot her, just to keep her from starving to death while she bounced.

Bill was never the same after that. He tried to forget about Slue-Foot Sue, but he was powerful lonesome and unhappy. He took to drinking wolf poison, and just to make it stronger, he'd mix a few fish hooks and some barbed wire into it. Uncle Joe said it was the fish hooks that finally done him in. They plum rusted out his insides, and that was the end of Pecos Bill. He weighed no more'n a mere two tons when he died.

Now, there are some pesky coyotes who don't for a minute believe this is *really* how Bill died. Why, I'm not even going to tell you what they think. If Uncle Joe says a thing is so, that's good enough for me, Pete the coyote! My Uncle Joe only tells true stories, and so, I believe him. Don't you?